'Now!' cried Sergeant Skinner, when he had judged that the canaries were close enough. The lightsmen leapt out of the bushes and swung their powerful torches upwards.

With split second timing, the canaries broke formation and scattered in all directions. The lightsmen stared round wildly, waving their lights in all directions. The canaries meanwhile had resumed attack formation and were now coming in fast and low from a completely different direction.

'Bombs away!' shouted Horace, releasing his tomatoes.

'Yay!' yelled the canaries, following his example.

The lightsmen swung round towards the noise, the netsmen lunged wildly, but it was too late. The canaries were already climbing steeply away from the danger area. The tomatoes, however, were still travelling at speed.

*Splatt! Splott!*

*Flying Squad* is the second in a series of adventures about a group of super-fit, super-strong canaries. The first title, *The Keep-Fit Canaries,* is also available in Corgi Yearling paperback.

D0610934

Also available by Jonathan Allen, and published by
Corgi Yearling Books:
THE KEEP-FIT CANARIES

# Flying Squad

## Jonathan Allen

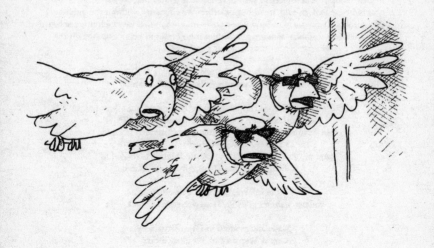

**CORGI YEARLING BOOKS**

FLYING SQUAD

A CORGI YEARLING BOOK : 0 440 863546

First publication in Great Britain

PRINTING HISTORY
Corgi Yearling edition published 1998
Reprinted 1998

Set in 13/16pt Bembo
by Phoenix Typesetting, Ilkley, West Yorkshire

Corgi Yearling Books are published by Transworld Publishers Ltd,
61–63 Uxbridge Road, Ealing, London W5 5SA,
in Australia by Transworld Publishers (Australia) Pty. Ltd,
15–25 Helles Avenue, Moorebank, NSW 2170,
and in New Zealand by Transworld Publishers (NZ) Ltd,
3 William Pickering Drive, Albany, Auckland.

For more information about Jonathan Allen,
contact website: HTTP://easyweb.easynet.co.uk/~jba

Made and printed in Great Britain by
Cox & Wyman Ltd, Reading, Berks.

# CHAPTER 1

## WHAT'S YELLOW AND HOT AND BOTHERED?

It was the sparrows who started it. If they hadn't told Neville the parrot about it, he wouldn't have got all worked up and rushed off to tell the canaries. *They* wouldn't have got even more worked up and vowed that, come what may, they were going to DO SOMETHING about it! And if they hadn't done *that*, there wouldn't be a story, and that would be a shame. So thank you, sparrows . . .

Before I start rattling on, I'd better take some time to fill in a bit of background for you. Neville is the Lord Mayor's parrot and the town's valued mascot. The seven canaries – Horace, Boris, Morris, Norris, Doris, Clarice and Alice – form his official bodyguard.

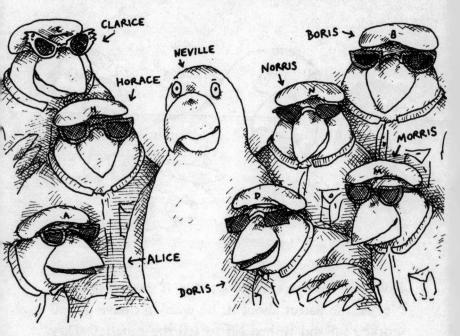

It's their job to look after him and, on State occasions, to fly in formation above him as he travels on the Lord Mayor's shoulder. It's a responsible job and they enjoy it, but this story finds them with something else on their minds.

'You mean they just put them in a crate without food and water and stick them on an aircraft?' Doris was incredulous. 'But that's *inhuman*, man!'

'Strange choice of word, that,' mused Morris. 'In*human*. That kind of behaviour is only *too* human if you ask me. Humans do that kind of thing all the time.'

'Yeah, yeah,' replied Doris impatiently. 'Point taken, but you know what I mean. I mean, it's cruel and evil. For instance, did you know that about three quarters of them die? Isn't that what you said, Neville?'

'At least three quarters,' agreed Neville, nodding gloomily. 'That's what the sparrows told me. They saw the programme last night through the TV shop window.'

'Well!' said Doris, hotly, 'what I want to know is, are we going to sit around protecting a pampered parrot from nothing in particular when our feathery brothers and sisters are being kidnapped and starved to death just because some human somewhere fancies an interesting pet?'

'*I am not pampered!*' cried Neville angrily. 'The very idea! I'll have you know . . .'

'All right, you lot, calm down!' interjected Horace. 'Nobody's going to sit around doing nothing. Not if I have anything to do with it. If only half of what those sparrows said is true then this is a very serious matter. And that's precisely why we can't rush into things. Any action we take needs to be carefully thought out. We can't just go and peck a few pet shop owners, however much you might feel like it, Doris. Anyway, the majority of them are completely innocent.'

'I'm for pecking them anyway!' muttered Boris.

'Luckily, I didn't hear that,' said Horace, giving Boris a look. 'We need to use our skill and intelligence,' he continued, 'to track down the guilty ones and bring them to justice.'

The others nodded. This sounded sensible.

Horace was the canaries' leader. He made a habit of being sensible. The canaries held him in great awe and respect. After all, it was Horace who had taken a group of rather grumpy caged canaries in a pet shop window, successfully planned their escape, and turned them into the famous, super-fit flying force they are today.

Of course, in case you hadn't guessed, the TV programme that provoked this strong reaction was a special report on the illegal trade in smuggled songbirds and other birds for pets. Many rare birds are threatened by this trade. These, and many not-so-rare birds, are kept and transported in appalling conditions in extreme heat and cold which cause many of them to die before they reach their destinations.

'The thing that shocks me,' said Horace, 'is the number of people prepared to pay large amounts of money for these rare species . . .'

'And the thing that gets *me*,' Doris added, 'is that these people probably think of themselves as bird lovers!'

'Well,' said Horace, 'if we're going to beat these smugglers, what we need is a plan . . .'

# CHAPTER 2

# WHAT'S YELLOW AND ALL EARS?

From the tree outside *Potter's Perfect Pets*, seven pairs of eyes scanned the street for any sign of activity. (Only seven because the canaries had managed to persuade Neville to stay at home. Even he had to agree that a large green parrot hanging around outside pet shops would excite the wrong sort of attention.) The street was deserted. All was quiet.

'All right, you know what to do,' whispered Horace. '*Go!*'

Two canaries – Boris and Norris – flew briskly down to the letter-box in the front door and, perching precariously, leaned on the flap until it opened a crack. A third canary – Clarice – pushed a small stick into the crack to hold it open while Boris and Norris shifted position and pushed harder. After a good deal of huffing and puffing, between them they managed to widen the crack until it was just big enough for something small, such as a canary like Alice, to squeeze through.

'Good luck, Alice,' called Horace. 'And don't forget the signal. We'll be back later to see how you're getting on. It might be a while; it depends how we get on at the other pet shops.'

Alice waved her wing in acknowledgement and, without further ado, slipped through the open flap and into the shop.

'Phew!' said Boris, once they had flown back to the tree. 'That was hard work. I hope they're not all like that.' He massaged his shoulder with his other wing. 'Remind me not to become a postman.'

'Boris,' said Doris.

'What?'

'Don't become a postman.'

'Eh?'

'Don't become a postman. I'm reminding you.'

'Oh, right, very funny,' said Boris sarcastically. 'You can do the next letter-box if you like.'

'No thanks,' retorted Doris. 'Us brainy types leave the heavy work to you brawny but dim types, know what I mean?'

13

Inside *Potter's Perfect Pets*, Alice let her eyes become accustomed to the light, or lack of it, then she flew over to the canary cage, opened the door and hopped in, shutting the door carefully behind her. Horace had taught the canaries all about cage doors and how to open them, and his strictly enforced fitness regime meant that they were all strong enough to deal with most of the cage doors they would ever come across.

'It's all right,' she whispered to the sleepy but startled canaries inside. 'It's all right, I'm a friend!'

There were five pet shops in the canaries' immediate area, and by nightfall each had an undercover canary inside, lying low amongst the shop's own stock of canaries. Luckily for Boris the other four had proved a lot easier to get into than the first.

This was the first part of Horace's plan – the gathering of information. He had figured out that the best way to find out about any possible illegal deliveries of smuggled songbirds was to infiltrate as many pet shops as possible, starting with the ones nearest home, and over the weeks move further out until they uncovered something suspicious. He hoped they wouldn't have to wait too long. So did Alice, Clarice, Doris, Norris and Morris . . .

# CHAPTER 3
# DORIS IS ON THE CASE

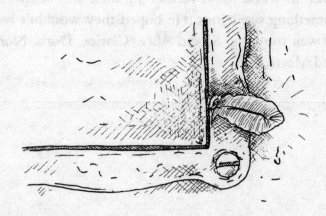

As luck would have it, Horace didn't have long to wait. Three days later, as Horace and Boris – on their pet shop patrol – flew by *Ace Songbirds, Pets and Supplies*, Boris noticed something. There was a tiny glint of colour at the bottom of the normally drab doorway and it definitely hadn't been there the last time they had flown past. They hurried down to investigate. Sure enough, there was a yellow feather stuck firmly in the side of the letter box. It was Doris's signal! She'd found something out!

Excitedly Horace and Boris held a quick meeting in a nearby bush.

'You attract her attention,' said Boris, 'and I'll check for a way out.'

'Good idea,' agreed Horace. 'There might be a window open or something.'

While Horace peered into the shop from the cover of the awning, Boris did a quick zoom round the building. He wasn't gone long.

'There's a small window open at the back,' he panted. 'She could get out of that, no bother.'

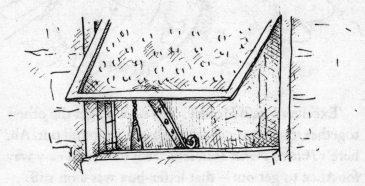

'Great!' said Horace. 'She's definitely seen me. I'll try and point to the back of the shop. I hope she understands what I'm getting at.' He turned and gestured animatedly through the glass, then he nudged Boris in the ribs. 'She's coming out!' he hissed. 'Go round to that window and make sure she's OK, will you?'

Boris flapped off round to the back of the shop.

Doris, when she appeared, was excited. 'There's something fishy going on!' she declared as the three canaries flew off. *'Definitely something dodgy in the offing here, no messing!'*

'Excellent!' said Horace. 'We need to get the others together, then you can tell us all you've found out. Ah, here's *Potter's Perfect Pets*, let's see if there's an easy way for Alice to get out – that letter-box was a bit stiff.'

'Yeah, well,' said Doris, 'just try and make sure that it's not through the toilet window, that's where I had to go. You realize that Frank Higgs, the pet shop owner, was in there, sitting on the loo reading his newspaper? I had to hold my breath and zip past his left ear to get out. You should have seen his face!'

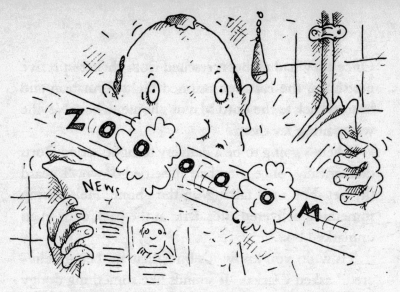

'Not as close as you saw it, thanks,' said Boris. 'But it's him I feel sorry for. Fancy seeing your face that close up when you're least expecting it! That would give anyone a turn.'

'If you were as funny as you are fat we'd all die laughing!' snorted Doris. 'But you're not, so don't worry about it.'

'Can you two give it a rest for five minutes!' exclaimed Horace. 'We've got work to do.'

Getting Alice out proved easier than getting her in. It was a hot day and the shopkeeper had wedged the door open to provide ventilation. All Alice had to do was choose her moment carefully to avoid being spotted, whip the cage door open and zoom out to join the others.

Once they had all been rescued from their respective pet shops, the canaries assumed flight formation and headed back to the Lord Mayor's house, where Neville was waiting for them.

'There's going to be a delivery tonight!' cried Doris dramatically, once they had all settled down. 'I heard the pet shop man talking on the phone. He's having something delivered after dark, at the back door in an unmarked box.'

'How do you know it's birds that are being delivered?' asked Clarice. 'It sounds like something dodgy but it might be anything. Dirty videos? Drugs even!'

'If you'll let me finish,' said Doris with an air of patient suffering, 'I'll tell you how I know. This is what I heard him say down the phone. He said, "Have you

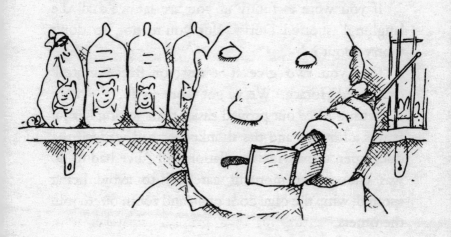

got them?" Then he said, "Right, so that's twenty pairs. Good, I've got customers waiting . . ." Then he had a bit of an argument about money, then he said, "It's a deal if you'll throw in the parrot as well." '

Neville bristled at this, '*Throw in the parrot*? I'll give him *throw in the parrot*! As if something as fine and noble as a parrot were some kind of afterthought! It's disgraceful!'

'So,' continued Doris, gesturing at Neville to be quiet, 'unless what we've got here is a late-night delivery of illegal underpants, I think we can safely assume that what he was talking about was birds!'

Horace was impressed.

'Nice work, Doris,' he said, patting her wing. 'It certainly sounds like a delivery of birds. Well,' he continued, setting his beak grimly, 'whatever it is, there's one thing for sure: there'll be seven canaries there to see it arrive!'

'And one parrot!' put in Neville. 'You're not leaving me behind this time!'

# CHAPTER 4

# PET SHOP PALAVER

It was nearly midnight, and at *Ace Songbirds, Pets and Supplies* all was quiet. The canaries, staking out the shop from a nearby tree, shuffled uneasily.

'Where's this delivery then?' muttered Boris. 'I'm getting cramp sitting here peering at that bloomin' shop. Who are they going to deliver whatever it is to anyway? There's nobody there!'

'Don't be so impatient, fatbeak!' hissed Doris. 'There's plenty of time.'

'Shhh!' said Horace. 'There's a car coming.'

'That's his car!' Doris informed them. 'I'd know Frank Higgs's old rustbucket anywhere.'

The car drew to a halt outside the shop and Frank Higgs, the shop's owner, got out. After looking carefully around he produced a bunch of keys, unlocked the door and went in.

'You see!' said Doris, kicking Boris. 'What's he doing here at this time of night if he's not expecting a delivery?'

'Ow!' said Boris.

'Can you two stop behaving like little chicks fighting over a worm!' scolded Horace. 'This is getting serious!'

A light went on at the back of the shop, followed by the sound of several bolts being drawn. There was a rattle, a squeak and a half-smothered cough. A pool of light spread out into the back yard, revealing an old washing-machine, a rotting shed and any amount of gently rusting corrugated iron.

'He's just opened the back door,' said Horace. 'Assume your watching positions. Neville, you stay here.'

'But you might need my special skills!' implored Neville.

Doris snorted. 'We're not that desperate!' she muttered under her breath. Neville had insisted on coming with them this time, so the canaries had to make sure he didn't mess things up. Neville meant well but he was inclined to be clumsy and not do what he was told. This made him a bit of a liability.

'But I want to see what's going on,' he moaned.

'We've been through that,' Horace reminded him patiently. 'You're just too conspicuous. A large, green parrot flying around late at night is a trifle unusual to say the least. No, Neville, you've got to stay here where nobody can see you.'

'He's just turned the light off,' Morris informed them. 'He doesn't want to draw attention to himself.'

'Right!' muttered Horace, 'let's get going.'

Frank Higgs lit another cigarette and scratched his ear. He leaned against the old washing-machine, which creaked unpleasantly. 'Come on, Terry!' he muttered under his breath. 'I haven't got all night.'

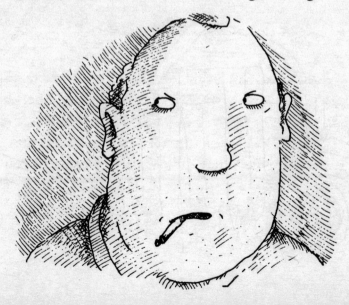

The sound of an approaching engine put him out of his misery. A small van was coming up the street. He ground out his cigarette on the long-suffering washing-machine and stepped forward. The van halted just outside and, at Frank's waved signal, began to reverse into the back yard.

'What took you so long?' Frank complained.

'I hit some traffic, didn't I?' whined Terry. 'And anyway, I couldn't go fast with this here precious cargo aboard, especially after that TV programme. Don't want to get stopped by the police, do I?'

'Yeah, all right,' grumbled Frank. 'Let's get them into the shop and have a look at them. They'd better be in good nick like you said or I don't want 'em.'

'Beautiful specimens, these!' Terry reassured him, 'considering where they came from. And wait 'til you see the parrot!'

As the two men carefully lifted the plain brown box out of the van, the watching and listening canaries could hear frantic flapping and the cheeping of small birds in distress coming from inside.

The canaries watched, grim-faced. They could barely control themselves but the knowledge that, unless they were patient, many more birds would suffer gave them strength.

'You guys are history!' swore Boris through gritted beak. 'I don't care how long it takes, but you're going to get it!'

'I'm with you on that one, big fella,' agreed Doris, 'but I want the big boys too. Horace, we've got to nail these scumbags!'

'We will,' said Horace, quietly. 'There's a change of plan. Norris, you fetch Neville. Come on, you lot, we're going for a ride!'

# CHAPTER 5

## MYSTERY TOUR

Terry's van was not in the first flush of youth, but that didn't stop him from driving like a maniac. The canaries and Neville, peering out from their hiding places in the back, pulled faces as they were rattled and bumped from side to side as another corner was negotiated just that bit too fast. They'd been driving for over two hours and all this shaking about was getting a bit wearing to say the least.

'What's he trying to do?' moaned Alice. 'Kill us all? Or is there something on the telly he wants to get home to see?'

'Roll over Damon Hill, here comes Terry!' muttered Morris.

'Where are we anyway?' enquired Boris. 'Street lights all look the same to me.'

'I've been noting the road signs,' said Horace from his perch near the rear window, 'and if it means anything to you, we are on the A317, thirteen miles south of Ipley.'

'Nope,' said Boris. 'Doesn't mean a thing.'

'I've never been so far from home,' Neville groaned, 'not since the Lord Mayor took me to the All-England Parrot Show eight years ago. But then of course I travelled in the official Mayoral car, not some clapped out old banger full of tatty bits of carpet and crushed beer cans.'

'Quiet everybody, we're turning off into a country lane,' said Horace urgently. 'Keep a look out for signs, and try to remember any turnings we take.'

Eight pairs of eyes scanned the roadside as the van sped along.

'We went left at the Queen's Head pub in Assingham,' shouted Norris.

'There was a humpback bridge over a stream at Weems,' noted Clarice.

'We're turning up a farm track,' pointed out Morris. 'Look, it says "New Farm". That should be easy to remember.'

The van bumped along, mercifully more slowly, until it swung into a farmyard where, at their approach, an unkempt dog of indistinct breed and uncertain temperament staggered to its feet, rattled its chain and gave a few half-hearted barks.

The farmhouse, despite its name, didn't *look* very new – although it must have been new once. The farmyard had the same air of long-term neglect. The rusting remains of what must once have been working farm machinery stuck out of the nettle bed that grew unchecked between two rickety barns. Generations of spiders had lived and died undisturbed in the cab of a large tractor which sat rotting half in and half out of an old chicken shed. There was no sign of any chickens.

There was no rosy-cheeked farmer leaning on his gate either. It wasn't that sort of farm.

However, there was an expensive-looking car parked round the other side of the farmhouse. As Terry got out of the van, a tall man in a suit appeared in the kitchen doorway and scowled at Terry.

'Got the money?' he asked, holding out his hand impatiently. 'Good, well hand it over and I can get out of this dump.'

'Here you go,' said Terry, handing him a wad of notes. 'Don't worry, it's all there. I know better than to try and rob you, Bernie.'

'It'd better be,' growled Bernie. 'Now remember, the big lorry's coming on the eighteenth at midday to take that lot.' He jerked his thumb in the direction of the first barn. 'You keep them sweet until then, got it?'

'Got it,' echoed Terry. 'You can rely on me, boss!'

'Good,' grunted Bernie. 'I'll be back on the eighteenth myself to supervise.'

With that, the man called Bernie got into his car and drove off, leaving Terry scowling after him.

'Yeah, yeah, boss!' muttered Terry. 'Whatever you say, oh great one!' He aimed a kick at the dog. It missed, the dog being well practised in the art of kick avoidance, and he went inside, still muttering.

# CHAPTER 6

# A DEPRESSING DISCOVERY

'What are we going to do now?' enquired Neville, once he was sure Terry had gone. 'I can't help noticing that we're stuck in the back of a dodgy old van in a strange farm miles from anywhere with no food or water. Not wanting to worry you or anything . . .'

'Don't worry, Neville,' said Boris, flexing his wings, 'this van is in such a state that if you sneezed loudly the doors would fall off.'

'You could use your special skills, Neville,' suggested Doris sarcastically.

'There are several rust holes we could get out of,' said Norris, looking around carefully. 'Not to mention the ventilator in the roof.'

'You're right,' agreed Horace. 'We won't try and get the back doors open, it would make too much noise. If we pick the gaffa tape off this hole by the wheel arch we could all get out, including Neville.'

'Good,' said Neville. 'Being that bit larger than you lot, I do tend to worry about getting stuck and suchlike.'

'Horace,' said Alice, once they were safely out of the van and in the shelter of the old tractor cab, 'what are we going to do now? What's the plan?'

'Yeah,' said Doris, 'I'm all for midnight drives into the country, but now we're here what do we do next?'

'I'll tell you,' said Horace. 'We are going to check out the old barn that the man called Bernie mentioned. I suspect we'll find something interesting in there. Something very interesting.'

He was right.

As they flew into the old barn, they caught their breath. It was stacked high with crudely made cages – cages of all shapes and sizes – and, as far as they could tell from the light thrown by the few dim light bulbs and by the variety of chirps, squeaks and squawks that greeted their ears, full of all kinds of birds.

'Phew!' gasped Morris, who didn't know whether to be impressed or appalled, or both. 'This is some operation! There must be a thousand birds in here . . .'

'At least,' agreed Horace, shaking his head. 'I had a feeling we'd find something like this. Parrots, finches, orioles, owls, hawks, you name it! I bet you this time last month they were free and happy in Africa, India, South America or the Caribbean. What a depressing sight!'

'I bet there were a lot more of them around when they started their journey, too!' put in Doris. 'A lot more.'

'Well,' said Horace, pulling himself together, 'we can't do anything to help them tonight. We need sleep and something to eat. There are some big bags of seed over in the corner – I noticed them as we came in. There's water, too. The best thing we can do is refresh ourselves for the morning. We'll need to be at our sharpest to help this lot.'

# CHAPTER 7

# WHAT'S YELLOW AND DEEP IN THOUGHT?

The morning found them much refreshed. They had managed to snatch some much needed sleep on a wide, comfortable beam, high up in the barn roof. There were a few bats up there, but they were friendly enough . . .

. . . Unlike the rats they had met by the bags of seed, who didn't see why they should let a bunch of little yellow birdies help themselves to what they saw as their seed. But even they saw reason eventually – especially after Boris and Neville had dangled their leader from a beam by his tail until he promised to leave them

alone. In fact, he was most accommodating. He told the canaries that they could eat as much seed as they liked whenever they liked, and would they mind putting him down as his tail hurt quite a bit and he didn't like heights very much and he'd always had the highest respect for canaries, always . . . er, and parrots of course, especially parrots!

Horace was perched on an old bicycle frame that someone had thrown up into the rafters many years ago. He was deep in thought. The other canaries watched him out of the corners of their eyes. They knew not to disturb him when he was working things out.

Eventually he stirred, shook his wings and beckoned to the others. They gathered round eagerly.

'Right!' he said. 'This is my plan . . .'

# CHAPTER 8

## WHAT'S YELLOW AND MISSING?

The Lord Mayor was worried.

'It's not like them to stay out late,' he told Inspector Jones. 'Especially my Neville. Normally they wouldn't miss their nine o'clock bath and bowl of sunflower seeds for the world, but last night they just didn't turn up. It was most distressing.'

'Hmmm,' said Inspector Jones, 'we'll have to see what we can do. I'll tell my men to keep their eyes open. We won't tell the press just yet. You never know, they might turn up at any moment, mightn't they?'

'I suppose so,' agreed the Lord Mayor reluctantly, 'but this has never happened before. I hope they haven't been kidnapped or murdered . . .'

'Now there's no need to get despondent, Your Worship,' said Inspector Jones. 'Those canaries can look after themselves.'

'That's true,' said the Lord Mayor, brightening. 'Perhaps they are just . . . er, unavoidably detained, so to speak. I just wish I knew that they were all right!'

'There'll be a van or a truck along soon, or maybe a car with a roof-rack or something,' Horace was saying, as he and Boris, Morris, Clarice and Doris settled into a suitable bush by the main road. 'If we wait here, by this junction, we could jump on as they slow down.'

'Couldn't we just fly back?' asked Clarice – she hadn't enjoyed the drive in the van the previous night.

'It would take too long,' said Horace, 'and besides, we'd be worn out by the time we got there. No, hitching a lift is the best way.'

'There's an open-topped truck coming,' observed Boris. 'Let's hope it's going the right way . . . Yes, it's indicating right. Come on, you lot. Last one on board's a linnet!'

# CHAPTER 9

# PREPARING THE GROUND

Back at the farm, Alice and Norris were in deep conversation with a group of sparrows.

'You lot are our heroes!' one of the sparrows was saying. 'We heard all about your sandwich snatching from our friends in town. We were dead impressed. We couldn't believe it when we realized that's who you were.'

'Thanks,' said Alice, embarrassed.

The canaries, after their ingenious escape from captivity, had become notorious for their daring sandwich snatches. Fierce canary pride had prevented them from grovelling after crumbs by the benches in the park. They had had enough of being fed by humans. No, they would get their meals *their* way, when *they* wanted them! Their fame had spread far and wide amongst both birds and humans.

The sparrows were suitably awestruck.

'What are you doing out here though?' asked a second sparrow. 'There's not a lot of food to snatch here, and there's nobody to snatch it from unless you count Terry, and you wouldn't want to snatch the stuff *he* eats!'

'Well,' said Alice, 'we're on an important rescue mission. Perhaps you'd be willing to help us. We'll need as many birds as we can get when the time comes!'

'Would we?' exclaimed the sparrow. 'I'll say we would. Tell us what you want us to do and we'll be right behind you. Give the word and I can get two hundred sparrows and maybe a few chaffinches and yellowhammers, all as tough as they come. No problem, it'll be our privilege to help!'

'Great!' said Norris. 'We'll provide you with the necessary basic training and, oh yes, one more thing . . .' Norris leaned forward. 'Do you know any woodpeckers?'

Inside the barn, Neville was fiddling with the door of the parrot cage.

'Hang on, nearly got it,' he was saying as he eased the catch upwards. 'That's it!' With a gentle ping it flipped undone and Neville slipped inside, where several astonished parrots regarded him in amazement.

'I know it must be a bit odd for you chaps to have someone breaking *into* a cage,' he began as he re-fastened the door, 'but it's all part of our cunning plan to rescue you and bring the villains that brought you here to justice.'

'Yeah?' said a sceptical sounding African Grey. 'Is that all?'

'It won't be easy,' continued Neville, striking an attitude, 'but if anyone can do it, we can!' He looked round suddenly. 'Ah, er . . . would someone mind giving me a hand? I seem to have shut my tail feathers in the door.'

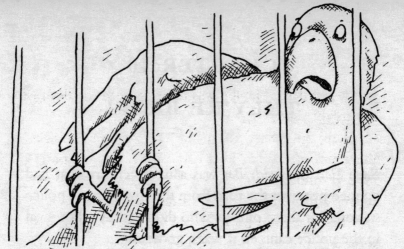

'Strewth!' said a cockatoo. 'Bloomin' Lord Muck here's goin' to rescue us. Don't he just inspire you with confidence?' He turned to Neville. 'All right, Mr Polly Parrot, or should I say Mr Pommie Parrot, how are you and your mates, whoever they might be, going to carry out this daring rescue then, eh?'

'Well, we're going to need your help,' began Neville. 'To start with, I'll need to lie low in your cage for a while, watch, listen and find out what I can.'

# CHAPTER 10

# THEY'RE BACK!

*Supa Eats Sandwich Bar* was a new venture that had opened just over the road from the town's main police station. For those officers who didn't fancy a hot meal in the police canteen it was a godsend.

WPC Yates certainly thought so. The smell of the fresh bread was too much for her as she stepped out of the door clutching her sandwiches in a paper bag: bacon, lettuce and avocado on granary bread, a classic combination. She was hungry, and she wasn't going to wait until she got back to the office; she was going to eat her sandwiches now!

Her mouth watered in anticipation as she fumbled with the bag. The lettuce looked fresh and enticing. She raised the sandwich to her mouth to take her first bite . . .

Suddenly there was a whoosh! A flash of yellow and no sandwich! All that remained was a small piece of lettuce spinning and twisting through the air. WPC Yates gaped in astonishment and shock. Then she let out a wail.

'My sandwich! Where's my sandwich?'

# CHAPTER 11

# WHAT'S YELLOW AND
# PREFERS POLICEMEN?

'I don't believe it!' cried Inspector Jones. 'Have they gone mad?' he groaned out loud as he held the telephone to his ear. 'Twelve times yesterday, and all policemen and policewomen? This is bizarre. Was the parrot with them? Oh, so there's still no sign of him then. What's that . . . ? Only five of them . . . ? And wearing dark glasses and berets you say . . . ? And those sleeveless jackets? Hmmm, this is not a good sign. Any clues on what's happened to the other two . . . ? Oh well, keep me informed . . . No, I'll talk to the Lord Mayor, he won't like this, he won't like this one bit.'

Inspector Jones sighed heavily as he put the phone down. The canaries were up to their sandwich-stealing tricks again! They seemed to have thrown in their job as bodyguards to the Lord Mayor's parrot, and resumed their lawless, food-filching ways, only this time, for some reason, there were only five of them.

The other odd thing was that they were targeting the town's police force. Why? Did they hold a grudge? Or, for mysterious reasons of their own, were they issuing a challenge to the forces of law and order? It was all most unfortunate. Inspector Jones well remembered the embarrassment he had felt last time as the special Canary Squad he had set up to try and catch the canaries had been thwarted time and time again. Made to look silly by a bunch of small songbirds.

'It'll be harder to catch them this time!' he groaned. 'I hope I'm not forced to re-form the Canary Squad; I don't want to put my job on the line for a bunch of canaries!'

'Well,' said Horace, 'that's got them wondering. What we need now is a bit of publicity; I think we should go after a few journalists now. The back garden at the Old Bull Inn is the most likely place. Come on, let's go!'

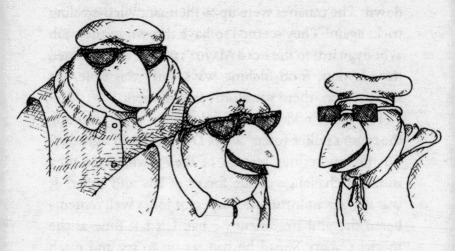

With a cheer, the canaries fell into formation behind him. With their berets and dark glasses, not to mention their special jackets with the sleeves pecked off, it was just like old times.

'Tell you what,' declared Doris, 'I'm enjoying this! I have to say that triple cheeseburger grab we did yesterday was a classic of its kind. The best bit,' she went on, 'was after we'd got the burger, when Boris insisted on going back for the salt and ketchup. Was that man cross! That was a laugh, wicked!'

'I can't eat a burger without ketchup,' said Boris. 'It's not the same somehow. That man was a chief inspector no less! He tried to hit me with the polystyrene box, but he missed. It was hilarious; his coleslaw went all down his jacket!'

'I remember that sticky toffee you swiped, Doris,' said Clarice. 'We wondered afterwards why you were so quiet, then we realized it was because you could hardly open your beak!'

'I had a nasty moment with that toffee,' remembered Doris. 'Birds' beaks just aren't designed to chew with. I wouldn't touch that stuff again if you paid me.'

'That's a shame,' said Boris. 'We finally find something that will shut you up and you won't touch it. It's not fair.'

'You're so funny, Boris,' said Doris sarcastically. 'You're so funny you should go on the stage. Then we could all come along and throw things at you.'

'Stop bickering, you little birdies!' scolded Horace. 'We're nearly there. Look, see that big bloke with the packet of pork scratchings? He's the sports editor. Let's zap him first, then we'll get the steak pie from the man who does the small ads. That should stir things up a bit!'

# CHAPTER 12

# WHAT'S YELLOW AND IN THE NEWS? AGAIN!

The Lord Mayor, as Inspector Jones had predicted, didn't like it. He didn't like it one bit. Not only had the canaries lost his beloved parrot, they had reverted to their old sandwich-snatching ways into the bargain. It made him angry to think that while his beloved Neville could be languishing, sick or injured or, worse still, in some dirty cage in a kidnapper's den, his supposed bodyguards were flaunting their feathers in the very face of the law itself. He was determined to do something about it.

'Jones,' he cried, getting to his feet as Inspector Jones came into his office, 'have you seen this?' He waved a copy of the morning newspaper in Inspector Jones's face. 'Have you? This provocation has got to stop! This is a slap in the face for my Mayoral authority. Attacking innocent men of the press at their innocent lunch! Depriving our brave bobbies of their necessary nutrition! Look at the headlines!'

Inspector Jones looked. Oh dear, he saw what the Lord Mayor meant:

FEATHERED FURIES IN SANDWICH SNATCH SHOCK

GUARD YOUR GRUB! THEY'RE BACK!

PRESS AND POLICE TARGETED IN FOOD FILCHING MAYHEM!

'Most unfortunate,' he muttered.

'Unfortunate?' cried the Lord Mayor. 'I'll say it's unfortunate. It'll be unfortunate for all of us if we don't catch those canaries pretty blooming quick. I want you to re-form the Canary Squad – that will keep the press quiet for a while – and I want my poor parrot found!'

'I'll see to it right away, Your Worship,' said Inspector Jones, groaning inwardly.

'FLYING YOBBOES' MUST BE STOPPED!

TOP COP GRUB SWIPE!

BOBBY BASHING BIRDIES MAKE A COMEBACK!

ANARCHY IN THE SKIES! POLICE AND REPORTERS IN THE FIRING LINE AS YELLOW PERIL RETURNS!

# CHAPTER 13

# AN OLD ADVERSARY

'So the whole town's buzzing,' said Doris. 'Now what? Do we do some more sandwich snatching? I haven't had so much fun in ages.'

'This isn't for fun, Doris,' said Horace. 'You know that. No, what we do next is wait and, if I'm right, we won't have to wait long.'

As Horace spoke, the canaries were flying over an important-looking square with statues of famous people waving swords, or standing nobly regarding the middle distance. On the wide-brimmed hat of one of the statues, a large white seagull watched them go by with great interest.

'Back to your old tricks, eh, little yellow birdies?' he muttered. 'Well, we can't have that, now can we?' He narrowed his eyes. 'Somebody I know would be very interested to hear about this,' he sniggered. 'Very interested indeed. He's big and he's bad and he doesn't like canaries. And guess who's going to tell him? Right now.' With that, the seagull flew off, chuckling like a villain in a bad old film.

# CHAPTER 14
# NEWS FROM AFAR

The next morning the canaries were doing their fitness exercises on their usual flat roof when a sparrow flew up.

'Hey, you lot, listen!' it yelled over the canaries' exercise music.

'Are you addressing us, small beak?' enquired Boris, haughtily. 'Have some respect! Do you know to whom you are speaking?'

'To whom?' mocked the sparrow. 'Respect?' He grinned at Boris. 'I respect the size of your stomach, mate! Listen . . .' he went on, ignoring Boris's protestations, 'I've got a message for you lot, all the way from the country, brought to you, from beak to beak, by Sparrow Express. It's from somewhere called New Farm.'

'A message from New Farm!' said Horace, gesturing the others to be quiet. 'This is important. Come on, sparrow, out with it.'

'The message is from Neville,' began the sparrow. 'He says the pick-up is on the sixteenth, not the eighteenth, but other than that all is well. Alice says the training is going to plan, but the woodpeckers are a bit noisy.'

'The sixteenth!' Horace was perturbed. 'That's tomorrow! We're going to have to get a move on! This is going to be tight.'

'Does that all make sense to you lot?' asked the sparrow. 'I hope so, because it don't make none to me.'

'Yes, it does,' said Horace, 'and thanks, you've given us vital information. Thank the other sparrows too, won't you.'

'I will,' promised the sparrow. 'Us sparrows are always glad to be of help. You know what they say, you can always rely on a sparrow.'

He hopped over to the edge of the flat roof and was about to fly away when he paused and frowned as if trying to remember something. 'Oh, yes,' he added,

slapping his forehead with his wing, 'that's what it was! Now, there was something I saw this morning that might interest you lot. I saw an old white van round the back of the police station. Men with nets and lights and stuff were climbing into it. They were arguing about who was going to hold the sandwiches or something. Guess what, it was that stupid Canary Squad. Remember them? 'Course you do.'

'Ah ha, so they've re-formed the Canary Squad!' said Horace, smiling grimly. 'Funny though it may sound, I'd been hoping they'd do that! In fact, I'm relying on it. Excellent!'

As the sparrow flew off, Horace paused to compose his thoughts, then clapped his wings.

'Attention, all canaries!' he cried dramatically. 'Things are happening fast. The Canary Squad has been re-formed, which is good news, but the bad news is that we've only got one more day to carry out Operation Wind-Up. Tomorrow is the sixteenth, which means that by the end of today that Canary Squad has got to be hopping mad! I want them hotter and crosser than a Lord Mayor with his regalia on fire!'

'Don't worry, man . . .' cried Doris, '. . . we'll wind them up so tight they'll be cross-eyed for a month!'

'Yeah,' added Morris. 'By the time we're finished, the steam from their ears will be visible two miles away!'

'That's the way,' said Horace encouragingly. 'Right! Turn that music off, and let's go!'

# CHAPTER 15

# THE PATHS OF NASTINESS
# REVISITED

The old church tower on the western outskirts of town was just as the seagull remembered it. The ivy had grown a bit more perhaps, but that was the only change. As he approached, a small flock of starlings flew out to check him over. These were no ordinary starlings; these were Sinister Starlings – servants and bodyguards to Nasty Nasty himself, identifiable by the eyepatch each wore on his right eye in honour of his master. As they approached, they seemed to recognize the seagull and sent two of their number back to the tower, hissing and twittering, to tell their master that he had a visitor. The rest fell silently into formation beside him.

Nasty Nasty was a large, black and white, ex-police falcon who had 'gone a bit weird', as Sergeant Cummings, his ex-handler, had put it. He wore an eyepatch with the letters NN picked out on it in diamonds and several heavy gold rings round his ankles. He lived in the old, mysterious church tower, surrounded by his faithful, if none too bright, Sinister Starlings. He was seldom found out and about.

As the seagull entered, he stood up on his special perch, spread his wings to their full extent and clicked his beak in annoyance. He wasn't in a good mood. He didn't like being disturbed.

'What brings you to the paths of Nastiness?' he asked in his high whining voice, the light glinting off the diamonds in his eyepatch. 'What news could a common seagull bring that could possibly be of interest to one such as Nasty Nasty?'

'You'd be surprised,' said the seagull boldly. 'I've got some information which might just make your day.'

'It would need to be pretty special to do that, seagull,' said Nasty Nasty quietly. 'I do hope you're not going to disappoint me! I hate being disappointed. When I'm disappointed I can turn . . . how shall I put it . . . ? Nasty!' He glared at the seagull with his good eye. The seagull swallowed hard and shuffled his feet nervously.

'It's those . . . er . . . canaries,' he began. There was a sharp intake of breath from Nasty Nasty. The Sinister Starlings covered their ears with their wings and cowered on their perch. He had mentioned the unmentionable!

'They're back on the streets,' the seagull went on. 'They're not under the protection of the Lord Mayor any more because they've given up their job.' He leaned forward. 'What I'm saying is . . . they're fair game!'

Nasty Nasty had relaxed and was grinning wickedly. The Sinister Starlings uncovered their ears and nudged each other.

'If they had some kind of . . . er . . . accident, shall we say,' continued the seagull, 'nobody would ask questions. In fact, even the Lord Mayor wouldn't be too upset. You see, they've lost his parrot!'

# CHAPTER 16

# THE TRAP IS BAITED

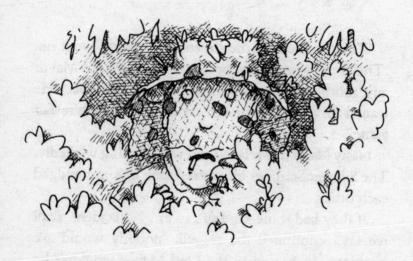

The Canary Squad van was parked cunningly under an overhanging tree to hide it from view. From above it would be pretty hard to spot. The netsmen and lightsmen, wearing their special camouflage hats, lurked in the nearby bushes – if you can call sitting on the ground looking bored, smoking cigarettes or picking your nose lurking, that is.

The plan was that a policeman sat himself in a conspicuous public place with an appetising-looking sandwich which he pretended to eat. The lightsmen lurked nearby, ready to leap out with their powerful lights and dazzle any approaching canaries intent on snatching the aforementioned sandwich. The netsmen would then catch the temporarily blinded and confused canaries in their nets.

It sounded simple.

It was simple, but it didn't work.

Well, all right, it had worked once but it had an enormously high failure rate. Nevertheless, in view of the high number of police-related sandwich snatches recently, they decided to persevere. You never knew, it might just work again.

The tomatoes at the front of Eileen Grove's vegetable stall were past their best. That's why they were on special offer. She expected them to go quite quickly. But she didn't expect them to go quite as quickly as they did . . .

She had just put the price ticket on the box when there was a whooosh! a flash of yellow, and half the tomatoes had disappeared.

'What the . . .' gasped Eileen in astonishment. 'It wasn't . . . it was! Bloomin' birds!' she exclaimed. 'How odd,' she added, after a moment's thought. 'Since when have canaries eaten overripe tomatoes?'

'Yellow Alert!' cried Sergeant Skinner of the Canary Squad, staring intently at a flashing light on the radar screen in front of him. The squad van had a specially sensitive radar inside it that could detect flocks of birds approaching. It had picked up a small flock flying in close formation in the immediate area. This small flock was heading their way at some speed and losing height at the same time. This was classic canary attack behaviour. The 'Yellow Alert' button flashed frantically.

'They're diving!' he shouted to the waiting lightsmen and netsmen. 'Stand by!'

Squinting up at the sky, the lightsmen could just make out five small dots. They seemed to be in formation, and they were getting larger. They tightened their grip on their lights, while the netsmen tensed their muscles, ready to spring.

'Now!' cried Sergeant Skinner, when he had judged that the canaries were close enough. The lightsmen leapt out of the bushes and swung their powerful torches upwards.

With split second timing, the canaries broke formation and scattered in all directions. Where were they? The lightsmen stared round wildly, waving their lights in all directions. The canaries meanwhile had resumed attack formation and were now coming in fast and low from a completely different direction.

'Bombs away!' shouted Horace, releasing his tomatoes.

'Yay!' yelled the canaries, following his example.

The lightsmen swung round towards the noise, the netsmen lunged wildly, but it was too late. The canaries were already climbing steeply away from the danger area. The tomatoes, however, were still travelling at speed.

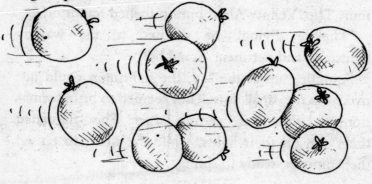

*Splatt! Splott!*

Ten overripe tomatoes splattered into a tangled mass of lightsmen and netsmen who, in the confusion, had collided with each other and were blundering about half blinded and tangled in nets. They were now half blinded, tangled in nets and covered in squashy bits of overripe tomato . . .

# CHAPTER 17

# WHAT'S BLUE AND SEEING RED?

There were quite a few Yellow Alerts that day. Some were false alarms. Some were deliberately triggered by the canaries who would then circle infuriatingly just out of reach of the lightsmen's lights. And some were genuine canary attacks. The Canary Squad never knew what was coming next. They had eggs dropped on them. A water bomb (a balloon Clarice had found, filled with water) was dropped with pinpoint accuracy into the back of the van, nearly blowing up the radar. A bag of flour burst smack in the middle of the bush the netsmen were hiding in. A pot of luminous orange paint hit the van, making it somewhat more conspicuous to say the least. They even had the van's tyres let down. (Boris had sneaked up and jammed pieces of gravel into the air valves.) They blamed this on kids, as they couldn't work out how a canary could have done it. The final straw was when the policeman acting as bait was sitting down to actually eat the sandwiches he had brought with him for lunch and the canaries, who had sneaked into range at ground level from a nearby street to avoid radar detection, zoomed in and grabbed the lot. To a man, the Canary Squad was fuming.

'I think that's enough,' said Horace from the canary's observation perch overlooking the square where the Canary Squad van sat in a pool of luminous orange paint. Around it, several flour- and tomato-covered policemen were busy pumping up the tyres and swearing at each other, the van, and the world in general.

'They look a bit hot and bothered, don't they?' said Boris. 'Can't think why . . .'

'They should be flattered that we're paying them so much attention!' grinned Doris. 'Some people just aren't satisfied.'

'Well,' said Horace, 'this is where it gets a bit more tricky . . .'

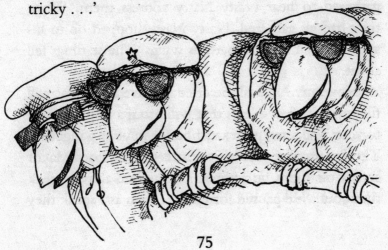

# CHAPTER 18

# SINISTER GATHERING

In the old church tower, the air rang with twittering, hissing and sinister laughter as the Sinister Starlings gathered to hear Nasty Nasty address them. When they had all gathered, Nasty Nasty hopped on to his special perch and clapped his wings. The starlings fell silent.

'Now, my Nasties!' he cried. 'I have news that will fill you with joy. News that will bring a twisted smile to your beaks and put extra bounce in your wingbeats. The canaries are back on the streets! The Lord Mayor smiles on them no longer. The police actively seek them out!' He paused for effect. 'Even as I speak they are being hunted down for unashamed and unprovoked sandwich snatching.' The diamonds on his eyepatch glittered unpleasantly. 'The canaries are vulnerable once more,' he continued, 'and that being the case, why should we not hunt them also? Why should we not take our chance? Should we not seek out these errant canaries? Seek out and DESTROY?'

The Sinister Starlings hissed and twittered their approval.

# CHAPTER 19

# THE TRICKY BIT

A large lorry marked *Ipley Haulage Ltd* drew up by the edge of the square. The driver jumped out, and disappeared into a nearby newsagent's. The canaries regarded the lorry with interest from a nearby tree.

'This is probably the best chance we'll get,' said Horace. 'We'd better give it a go. Doris, you nip over and attract their attention – they'll have fixed the tyres by now.'

As Doris flew off, the others positioned themselves conspicuously by a gap in the tarpaulin which covered the lorry's load.

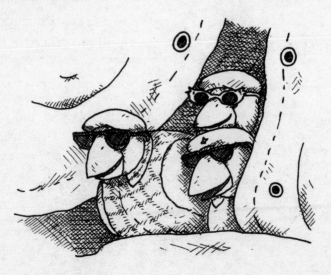

Constable Jim Cross, one of the flour-dusted netsmen, was sitting in a depressed huddle under a tree near the Canary Squad van. He was catching his breath after pumping up the van's tyres and trying to scrub some of the luminous orange paint off the windscreen. He glanced up into the tree above his head, and froze. Something yellow was moving about in the branches. He watched with intense concentration as the yellow something flitted to the next tree. It was a canary! And it was wearing a beret and dark glasses! He signalled to his colleagues to attract their attention, put his finger to his lips and pointed to the tree with the canary in it.

Obligingly it flew to the next tree and carefully, trying not to be seen, the Canary Squad followed.

'It's all right, it hasn't seen us,' whispered Constable Cross. 'It's in that tree above that lorry there . . .'

'Look!' Constable Williams, a netsman (with a fair amount of tomato still adhering to his uniform), stifled a cry. 'Look, on the lorry! It's the others, and they're hopping around that gap in the tarpaulin there.'

'They've sneaked into it!' hissed Constable McHugh, who had joined them behind their bush. 'Are they going to hitch a ride or something?'

'Looks like it,' said Constable Cross. 'The lorry's starting up! Quick! Get back to the squad van. We're going to follow it! Wherever they're going, we're going too! Get on the radio and tell Control what we're doing. And ask for some assistance.'

Sergeant Cummings, late of the Canary Squad, had been transferred to the Motorcycle Patrol division. He loved his new job, but had nevertheless paid close attention to the canaries' recent behaviour. It made him angry to learn that they were out on the streets once more, flaunting the law of the land and victimizing his colleagues.

'They'd better not try that sandwich-snatching lark with me!' he muttered darkly.

So when the message came over the radio that the Canary Squad was asking for assistance, he spun his motorbike in a spectacular turn and screeched off to give what help he could.

# CHAPTER 20

# THE YELLOW LEADING THE BLUE?

In the sky, high above the square, a small flock of sinister-looking birds were circling slowly. Nasty Nasty, with his hawk's super eyesight, had located the canaries just as they were disappearing under the tarpaulin.

'Curses!' he whined. 'Those yellow vilenesses are hitching a lift! The Canary Squad van is following. We must do likewise!'

The sound of a noisy motorbike taking a corner too fast jerked his attention to the other side of the square. Sergeant Cummings zoomed into view. He slowed when he saw the Canary Squad van moving off ahead of him. It was following a large lorry with *Ipley Haulage Ltd* written on the side. He tucked in behind the van and gave a short wave to Constable Cross, who gave him the thumbs up salute from the rear window.

'Aha!' cried Nasty Nasty. 'I'd recognize that ugly face anywhere. Sergeant Cummings, as I live and breathe!' Sergeant Cummings had been the official Police Hawk-Handler back in the days of Nasty Nasty's police service. Nasty Nasty remembered him well.

'Well, my Sinister Starlings,' he murmured, 'you and I shall hitch a lift . . .'

Clarice peered carefully out from the canaries' hide-away under the tarpaulin.

'They're still there,' she reassured Horace, 'and judging from that last road sign, we're on the Ipley Road about five miles from Corborough.'

'OK,' said Horace, 'we'll jump off at the round-about with the A362. We should be able to hop on to something going up the Assingham Road. If not we'll just have to do a bit of flying until something comes along. It's important that we're seen, but we have to make it look as though we don't know we're being followed.'

At the roundabout, the only vehicle going up the Assingham Road was a small open-topped sports car. Much to Doris's disappointment, Horace vetoed this on the grounds that it would go too fast and lose the Canary Squad van, and what would be the point of that? Reluctantly, Doris had to concede.

'There's a lorry full of manure coming!' put in Clarice helpfully.

Doris groaned. 'Oh great!' she cried. 'Thank you, Clarice, now we can really travel in style!'

'Perfect,' said Horace. 'Come on, you lot, hop on board. Don't worry, Doris, this won't be for long.' Muttering darkly, Doris followed the others on to the lorry.

'They're going up the Assingham Road!' cried Constable McHugh. 'They've swapped vehicles and they're turning left up there!' He pointed after the manure lorry chugging towards Assingham.

The Canary Squad van turned hurriedly, followed by Sergeant Cummings on his motorbike.

'There's something funny about Cummings's motorbike,' said Constable Cross, staring out of the back window of the van. 'I couldn't work it out earlier, but now he's nearer, I can see. It looks as if he's covered in birds!'

'Eh?' said Constable Williams, joining him at the
window. 'Wow!' he exclaimed. 'How odd. Look at
that great big hawk sitting on his handlebars!'

'Hawk, you say?' asked Constable Block. 'He used
to be a police hawk-handler a few years back,
Cummings did. A big black and white job it was,
vicious too. They used it to keep pigeons off the Town
Hall until it went a bit weird.'

'It looks like Cummings has gone a bit weird if
you ask me,' said Constable Cross. 'I've never seen
anything like it!'

86

'Talking of birds,' put in Constable McHugh, 'I could swear I just saw a flock of sparrows flying in formation! And the weirdest part was, they were chasing a cat!'

'This is all getting a bit strange,' said Constable Williams.

'They've jumped off the lorry and now they're flying up that farm track!' Constable McHugh informed them. 'What do you want me to do? Shall I follow?'

'Best not,' advised Constable Williams. 'They'll know they've been followed. Park out of sight in these woods here, and we'll go up on foot.'

# CHAPTER 21

# REVOLUTION AT NEW FARM

Up at New Farm there was no sign of life. Human life, that is. Terry and his dog were engaged elsewhere, as they usually were in the afternoons, the betting shop being open all day . . . There was plenty of activity on the bird front though. A flock of very fit and organized-looking sparrows were on lookout duty in a nearby tree.

'All present and correct, awaiting your arrival, sir!' cried their leader, landing in front of Horace and saluting.

'Er . . . very good,' said Horace, not knowing quite how to react. 'Very nice berets – er, where did you get them from?' he asked, noticing the sparrows' headgear.

'Some of the small finches have been making them for us out of old grain-bags. It was Alice's idea,' replied the sparrow. 'We couldn't get hold of any dark glasses though. It's a real shame,' he added.

'Where are Alice, Norris and Neville?' asked Horace. 'There's been some serious organizing going on. I'm impressed.'

'Alice is out with number three squadron on a Cat Awareness Exercise,' said the sparrow, 'and Norris and Neville are in the barn organizing the woodpeckers.'

As the sparrow spoke, a loud drumming sound came from the direction of the barn.

'I'll fetch them,' said the sparrow.

'No need,' said Horace quickly. 'We'll go in and find them. Can you stay here,' he added, 'and watch the drive? If you see a bunch of policemen approaching, send someone in to tell me.'

'Yes, sir!' said the sparrow, saluting again.

In the barn they found Norris and Neville directing a couple of woodpeckers as they cut neatly round the hinges of the largest parrot cage.

'You got the message then?' said Neville, looking up as Horace approached. 'As you can see, we're working flat out to get everything ready for tomorrow. The woodpeckers have been marvellous. Norris's idea, that,' he added generously.

'Tremendous!' said Horace, impressed. 'You have been busy.'

'Once we've done this cage, that will be everything finished,' said Norris. 'It's been hard work, but the woodpeckers here agreed to do their bit for our cause. We've got a food squad who go out and find grubs for them to eat, so they don't go hungry.'

'Glad to help,' said one of the woodpeckers, spitting sawdust out of his beak. 'Excuse me!'

'Alice has done wonders with the sparrows,' said Norris. 'They've really taken to their training programme. It's great to work with them, they're so enthusiastic!'

'I noticed that,' agreed Horace. 'They looked pretty fit, too.'

Just then a sparrow flew in with an urgent message for Horace. 'There's a bunch of policemen creeping up the drive,' he informed him. 'They seem to be covered in flour or something. There's also a flock of strange birds clustered round a motorbike. They're coming this way too.'

'Uh-oh,' said Horace, 'this is a complication I didn't expect.'

'Who are these motorcyclist-friendly birds then?' asked Boris. 'Anyone we know?'

'In a way,' replied Horace. 'I'll explain later. The best thing we can all do now is hide up in the rafters and watch.'

# CHAPTER 22

# THE GUESTS ARRIVE

'There's nobody about,' whispered Constable Cross, peering through the farmhouse windows.

'Why are you whispering then?' said Constable McHugh in his normal voice, nudging him.

'Let's see what's in those barns,' suggested Constable Williams. 'I bet that's where those canaries are hiding.'

The Canary Squad crept carefully into the barn just as Sergeant Cummings and Nasty Nasty swept into the farmyard.

'Spread out and search, my Sinister Starlings!' cried Nasty Nasty. 'Those yellow devils can't be far away!'

'Well, well,' said Sergeant Cummings, taking off his helmet, 'this is a scruffy old place you've brought me to and no mistake, you strange old bird you.' He reached out to pat Nasty Nasty as he would have done in the old days, but something in the falcon's eyes made him draw his hand back. 'Ah well,' he muttered to himself. 'Times change; times change . . . I'd better have a look round and see where the others have got to.'

In the big barn, the Canary Squad were standing, open-mouthed, staring at the lines of cages stretching before them. Constable Williams whistled.

'Phew! What a lot of birds,' he muttered. 'What are they doing stuck away in this old barn?'

'It looks dead suspicious to me,' said Constable Block, peering into the nearest cage. 'I bet these are all rare smuggled birds or something.'

'I saw a TV programme all about that caper!' exclaimed Constable McHugh. 'It's a highly organized business apparently,' he went on. 'A lot of money changes hands.'

'This looks highly organized to me,' observed Constable Cross. 'There are some exotic-looking specimens here. You know what? I think we've stumbled on the headquarters of a bird-smuggling gang!'

'Maybe not the headquarters,' Constable McHugh corrected him. 'This is probably just where they store the goods before distributing them to collectors and other dodgy characters who aren't going to ask questions.'

'We need to radio headquarters about this,' said Constable Williams. 'This is big!'

'I'll do that,' said Constable McHugh. 'I'm glad we parked the van out of sight. I'll tell Cummings to hide his motorbike; we don't want to alarm whoever is in charge of this lot.'

'We'll conceal ourselves in here,' said Constable Block. 'All we can do is wait for reinforcements to arrive. Tell them to be inconspicuous if they can manage that.'

# CHAPTER 23

## NASTY NASTY TURNS NASTY

'Did you hear that?' asked Boris, peering down from his beam in the rafters. 'They just *happen* to have stumbled across this lot! What a cheek! We had to practically take them by the hand and drag them!'

'Well, at least we got them here,' said Doris, 'though what good that sorry bunch are going to do is debatable.'

'At least they did the sensible thing and rang for re-inforcements,' said Horace. 'Uh oh, here comes trouble . . . Keep your heads down!'

He had caught sight of a small group of Sinister Starlings who had just flown into the barn and were hopping about in agitation, hissing and twittering amongst themselves. One of them flew out again while the others explored the barn, examining the cages and shaking their heads.

A moment later, the gentle twittering of the small caged birds stopped dead as a dark and deadly shape swooped into the barn.

'Cages!' hissed Nasty Nasty in distaste as he took in the scene. 'Row upon row of cages!' He shuddered as he glided across the barn to perch on a low beam. He gave a sharp intake of breath as his eye was caught by a large cage nearby. He let out a high, chilling scream. The cage was full of rare falcons.

'My brothers!' he shrieked. 'Caged like common songbirds!' He flew down to the cage and began to tug at the bars ineffectually.

'Who did this to you?' he cried. 'What manner of being would lock away the cream of birdkind in this unspeakable way?' He narrowed his eyes. 'They shall suffer!' he swore. 'The perpetrators of this deed shall suffer torments. I, Nasty Nasty, swear it!'

'Lays it on a bit thick, doesn't he?' whispered Boris to Horace, as they watched from the safety of their beam.

'This might just work in our favour . . .' muttered Horace. 'You lot stay out of sight. I'm going down there.'

'You can't do that!' hissed Morris. 'That big hawk is dangerous. Even a super-fit canary is no match for him and his Sinister Starlings!'

'Trust me,' said Horace. 'I am not going to wrestle with him, I'm going to talk to him. I know it's a risk, but trust me!'

So saying he swooped down and perched on a conspicuous beam, a safe distance away from Nasty Nasty. He coughed. The Sinister Starlings and Nasty Nasty looked up. Before they could react, Horace spoke.

'We've had our differences, Nasty Nasty, you and I,' he declared, 'but today we have a common purpose. The canaries and I have been planning for weeks to bring these bird-smugglers to justice. You can help,' he said simply. 'Together we could be a very powerful force. What do you say?'

Nasty Nasty drew himself slowly up to his full height. 'I say that for a small songbird you have a lot of nerve,' he growled, regarding Horace coldly with his visible eye. 'You wish me, Nasty Nasty, to join with your sad bunch of disgraced canaries!'

'Let him tell you his plan,' interrupted a voice from the falcon's cage. 'It just might work. Us falcons are on his side, and so is every bird in this place.' There was a general twittering and squawking of agreement throughout the barn. Nasty Nasty raised his eyebrows.

'Well, in view of that vote of confidence from an unexpected quarter' – he inclined his head towards the falcon cage – 'I suppose I had better hear you out. Enlighten me, what form does this plan take, o small yellow one?'

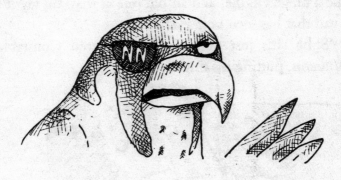

# CHAPTER 24

# THE CANARY SQUAD STRIKE!

Sergeant Cummings had just hidden his motorbike behind an old combine harvester when he became aware of the sound of an engine approaching from the direction of the farm track. Ducking down low, he sprinted for the cover of the barn.

'Car coming!' he hissed as he threw himself down behind a stack of large cages where the rest of the Canary Squad were hiding.

'It's not the Ipley police come to help?' enquired Constable McHugh.

'No!' whispered Sergeant Cummings. 'It sounded like a diesel engine, and an old one at that. I'd say it's a van that has seen better days.'

'Shhh! It's just pulled up!' whispered Constable Williams, putting his finger to his lips.

'Well, here we are, boys!' said Terry, slamming the van door, causing a small shower of rust particles to cascade on to his left foot. 'Here we are in this beautiful rural location,' he continued, 'knee deep in golden corn and cider apples et cetera.'

'Too right!' agreed a small, balding man called Ron, looking around and shaking his head. 'Don't forget the fat speckled hens clucking contentedly in the hayloft.'

'Oh, shut up, you lot!' growled Percy, the van's other passenger, as he clambered out. 'It's bad enough having to come out to this dump at the height of the hay fever season without listening to you idiots trying to be funny!'

'Ooh! Who rattled the bars of your cage?' mocked Ron. 'We're just having a bit of fun. Which isn't easy with a miserable so and so like you moping about like a lost walrus.'

'Like a what?' asked Percy.

'Come on, come and look at what you've got to shift tomorrow,' said Terry, interrupting a potential argument. 'That'll cheer you up!'

In the barn, Sergeant Cummings and the Canary Squad held their breath. They could hear Percy moaning and Ron teasing him as the men approached.

'There's only three of them!' whispered Sergeant Cummings. 'And there's five of us. We could handle this ourselves!'

'As long as they're not armed!' Constable Cross whispered back.

'Have you ever heard of armed bird-smugglers?' replied Sergeant Cummings. 'Why would a bird-smuggler need a gun?'

Constable Cross pulled a face and shrugged.

'All right then,' Sergeant Cummings continued, 'when I give the signal, we jump on them!'

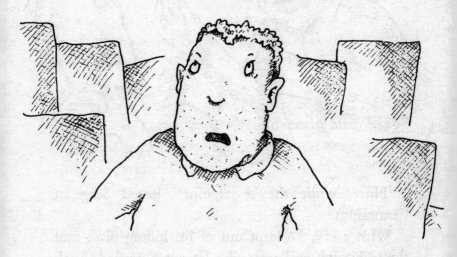

'What, all this lot?' moaned Percy, when he saw the stacks of cages. 'This isn't going to do my back any good at all, this isn't!'

'Something wrong with your back is there?' Ron enquired. 'Is there any part of you that's not defective in some way?'

'It's all right for you short fat people!' replied Percy. 'You don't get any back problems.'

'I am not fat!' cried Ron hotly, going red in the face.

'Now, while they're arguing!' hissed Sergeant Cummings.

With a cry, he leapt out of his hiding place and threw himself at Terry, who let out a startled shriek and fell to the ground, Sergeant Cummings on top of him.

The surprise was complete; Percy and Ron didn't even struggle when Constable Cross and Constable Williams grabbed them.

'Get the handcuffs on them!' cried Sergeant Cummings, getting his breath back. 'You lot are nicked!'

# CHAPTER 25

# NOT SO FAST . . .

'I don't think so,' interrupted a calm voice from the barn doorway. 'I don't think so at all. Put the handcuffs away and put up your hands; this is not a pea-shooter.'

The man called Bernie, he of the flash car and the gruff manner, stepped forward, gun in hand. He had arrived unexpectedly early. He hadn't been due until the next day, the day when the big lorry would come to take the cages away up north. But he had wanted to check that everything was in order. He didn't entirely trust Terry. It seemed that he had arrived in the nick of time . . .

Beside him in the doorway stood the grinning figure of Steve, his bodyguard and right-hand man. Steve's right hand had a gun in it, too. The noise of their arrival had been masked by the noise of the scuffle.

'Steve,' said Bernie, 'how would you like to hand-cuff these tomato-stained and lightly floured coppers together and put them in the back of Terry's van?'

Steve's grin widened. 'A pleasure, boss!' he smirked, putting his gun away. 'A very great pleasure! What have you lot been doing?' he asked as he handcuffed the hapless Canary Squad. 'Making pizzas?'

Ron and Terry sniggered.

Constable Cross looked at Sergeant Cummings. 'Whoever heard of an armed bird-smuggler?' he muttered, under his breath.

Sergeant Cummings scowled.

Up in the rafters, Horace took in the scene.

'We're going to have to do something about this!' he said to himself grimly. 'The moment has come for Operation Free as a Bird!'

# CHAPTER 26
# THE BATTLE OF THE BARN

Suddenly, before Horace could give his signal, there was a shriek of rage from the other side of the barn.

Bernie looked up, startled. A huge hawk was speeding towards him, talons outstretched. Behind him streamed a line of grim-faced Sinister Starlings.

'The idiot!' cried Horace. 'Why couldn't he wait for the signal? Oh well, here goes!' He took a deep breath and launched himself off the beam.

'Freedom!' he cried. This was the signal all the other birds had been waiting for.

Instinctively, Bernie raised the gun and pointed it at the approaching falcon. But before he could fire there was a flash of yellow and brown, and the gun was knocked clean out of his hand. It was Alice and her squadron of sparrows, arriving in the nick of time. Bernie howled as, a split second later, Nasty Nasty careered into him, knocking him off balance. Steve struggled to get his gun back out of his pocket, but it was too late; Horace and the others were on him, pecking his fingers, while the Sinister Starlings, in a mad rage, flapped around him, screeching and scratching.

'Here we go, here we go, here we go!' sang the sparrows as they zoomed round the barn, preparing themselves for another attack. As they circled they were joined by a stream of birds of all shapes and sizes from the cages below. The cage doors which the woodpeckers had weakened crashed to the ground as the caged birds knocked them out and escaped to help the struggle. Neville flapped about, organizing them. When they were all gathered in a great flock, he gave the signal and they charged . . . It was an awesome sight!

Apart from a potentially dangerous situation when Ron grabbed a broom and was about to flail it around his head at the attacking birds, it was no contest really. The day was saved by a group of American woodpeckers who drilled through the broom-handle in four

places. No, the bird-smugglers didn't stand a chance. Before they could move again, a cloud of birds engulfed them and, within two minutes, they were cowering in a corner, covering their heads with their hands or with their coats – all except Percy, who lay on the ground shouting, 'Get away from me, I'm allergic to feathers!'

At a signal from Horace, the birds fell back. Once the birds were out of the way, the Canary Squad jumped on the bird-smugglers and handcuffed them securely. It was all over.

Except for a commotion going on in one corner of the barn . . .

'You can't get away from me that easily!' a muffled squawking voice was shouting. Everybody looked around. A discarded jacket was flapping and writhing on the floor as if it had a life of its own.

'Take that!' cried the voice. 'And that!'

Sergeant Cummings reached down and turned the jacket over, revealing Neville, rolling and writhing, his head stuck firmly in the inside pocket. He laughed.

'Neville!' said Horace, flying down and patting him on the back. 'Neville! Calm down, soldier. It's all over. Calm down!'

'What?' panted Neville, disentangling himself. 'Where's he gone? I had him good and proper a minute ago.' He looked around in confusion.

The other birds simply laughed and cheered.

'Stupid bird!' muttered Bernie.

'There he is!' cried Neville, pointing with his wing. 'Who are you calling stupid?' Before anyone could stop him, he flew at Bernie and gave him an almighty peck on the nose. The other birds cheered even harder.

And now it really *was* all over.

# CHAPTER 27

## WINDING DOWN

Horace, Neville and the rest of the canaries flew here and there, trying to calm the more excitable birds and assessing any injuries that had been sustained. There were remarkably few, thankfully. The most serious were some greenfinches with concussion, some sparrows with cuts and bruises and, last but not least, Nasty Nasty himself, who had sustained a badly broken wing. He was being supported by a couple of Sinister Starlings and Alice, who was trying to organize some bandages.

'Tear some strips off those grain-bags and bring them over here!' she ordered. Several sparrows flew over to the grain-bags and began shredding them.

'Don't fuss so, birdy!' Nasty Nasty grumbled.

'Now be quiet and hold that wing still while I bandage it!' scolded Alice, as if talking to a naughty chick. Nasty Nasty shut up and held his wing still . . .

'Blimey!' muttered Boris. 'You don't mess with Alice! Did you see that?'

'Not half!' said Doris. 'She'll be telling him to eat up his nice birdseed next.'

Just then there was the sound of car doors slamming and excited voices outside. Twenty uniformed police officers burst into the barn and stopped, astonished. It was the Ipley police reinforcements, but they weren't needed.

117

# CHAPTER 28

# ALL'S WELL THAT ENDS WELL

Once the Lord Mayor was in full possession of the facts, it didn't take him long to work out why the canaries had behaved the way they did. He was impressed.

'They led your Canary Squad to the gang's hideout at considerable risk to themselves, and saved your boys from two desperate gunmen,' he told Inspector Jones. 'Then they rounded up the whole gang for your lot to arrest. A magnificent performance if you ask me!'

'Magnificent . . .' echoed Inspector Jones.

He wasn't gripped by the same degree of canary fever as His Worship, the Lord Mayor. His Canary Squad had been made to look very silly. A bunch of experienced police officers being dragged around the country by a small flock of canaries! The Canary Squad had made the arrests, which put them in a better light, but the whole world knew that without the canaries they wouldn't have managed it. No, even though they had made a number of arrests the next day when the big lorry turned up and, acting on information from the canaries, raided a number of pet shops, including *Ace Songbirds, Pets and Supplies*, and rescued many more rare birds, the police hadn't come out of this business in a very good light.

'I propose that you disband the Canary Squad,' continued the Lord Mayor, 'and, using the officers involved, set up an anti-bird-smuggling unit. The Chief Constable agrees with me.'

Inspector Jones smiled fixedly.

'Oh, yes,' the Lord Mayor went on. 'You should reinstate that brave falcon. He may be a bit strange, but he could be a valuable addition to our anti-bird-smuggling initiative!'

'Well,' said Neville, 'here we are, back home again, and I have to say I'm not sorry!'

'I'm just glad it all worked out all right in the end,' said Horace, 'but it was worth the risk to get those bird-smugglers behind bars!'

'A masterpiece of planning, if you don't mind me saying so,' put in Alice. 'We may be small, compared to humans, but we can still show them a thing or two!'

'And what about Nasty Nasty?' said Boris. 'I'm just glad he was on our side!'

'Yeah,' said Doris, 'he may be a few eggs short of a full nest but he's all right by me.'

'You heard he's been made part of the anti-bird-smuggling unit?' said Norris.

'Well I guess it'll keep him out of trouble,' said Boris, 'but what are we going to do? We can help them out when they need it, but it's going to seem awfully quiet just sitting around looking after old Neville here.'

'Quiet?' said Doris. 'Since when has that great green squawker been quiet? I get a headache just looking at him!'

'That's rich coming from you!' retorted Neville. 'You rabbit on so much I'm surprised they don't build you a hutch in the garden!'

'Ooh, look who's talking?' cried Doris. 'I'm sorry, but I hadn't got you down as the strong and silent type.'

'Children, children!' admonished Horace, grinning.

Things were back to normal all right!

THE END

# ABOUT THE AUTHOR

Jonathan Allen was born in 1957 and went to school in Bedfordshire and Cambridgeshire before going on to do an Art Foundation Course in Cambridge. He has a degree in Graphic Design from St Martin's College of Art, and has been involved in illustration ever since graduating. Another of his lifelong interests is music. He used to play bass guitar and run a recording studio.

He has recently moved out of London to the Cambridgeshire countryside with his wife and two children, Isobel and Alasdair.

He has written over twenty children's books and his titles for Transworld include *Flying Squad* and *The Keep-Fit Canaries*, both published by Corgi Yearling Books and *Chicken Licken*, published by Picture Corgi Books.

If you'd like to know more, why not check out Jonathan Allen's website:

HTTP://easyweb.easynet.co.uk./~jba

Interested in *real* birds?
Send for your free copy of
*The Beak Fun Book* and
information on the YOC.

YOC is the junior membership of The Royal Society for the Protection of Birds and has over 150,000 members throughout Great Britain. Members can discover all sorts of interesting things about birds and wildlife, get the chance to take part in fun activities or explore over 100 nature reserves for free. And, every member receives the award-winning magazine, *Bird Life*, six times a year!

For further information and a copy of the Beak Fun booklet packed with fun, puzzles, games, jokes and facts about birds and other wildlife, complete the coupon (or copy it on to a separate piece of paper) and send to:
The Royal Society for the Protection of Birds, Department BFB 3493, The Lodge, Sandy, Bedfordshire SG19 2DL

..............................................................................................................

**Please rush me my FREE Beak Fun Book**
**(capital letters please)**

My name...........................................................................................

My address.......................................................................................

..............................................................................................................

..................................................................................postcode....................

My date of birth ...........................

I'm a member of the YOC: Yes...... No......
code BFB3493

*Registered Charity No. 207076*

# THE KEEP-FIT CANARIES

## Jonathan Allen

**The prequel to *Flying Squad***

What's yellow, fast and unbeatable?
Seven bolshy canaries, that's what!

Follow the hilarious and daring escapades of the brave
birdies who refuse to be confined to a cage!

**'Highly recommended'** *The School Librarian*

0 440 86293 0

# ROBOPOP

## Emma Laybourn

*'I don't want a robot for a father!' wailed Ben.*

When Ben's father – a robotics expert – has suddenly to go away over the half-term holiday, he has a big surprise for Ben: a very special robot to take his place . . . a robopop!

There's only one problem. Like lots of Dad's robots, this robot doesn't quite work as well as expected. And as one hilarious mishap follows another, Ben realizes this is going to be one half-term he will never forget!

0 440 86352 X

# OPERATION GADGETMAN!

## Malorie Blackman

Beans calls her dad 'Gadgetman' because of the weird and wonderful gadgets he comes up with – everything from exploding biscuits to Spy Kits. But when Gadgetman accidentally invents a device that could be used to steal millions of pounds, he is suddenly in terrible danger. The wrong people find out and Gadgetman goes missing – kidnapped!

Can Beans track down the kidnappers and find Gadgetman before he is forced to hand over details of his invention? With the help of her friends, Ann and Louisa, and her special Gadgetman Spy Kit, she is determined to try . . .

**From the author of the award–winning *Hacker*.**

**'Full of humour and excitement'** *Books for Keeps*

0 440 86307 4

# CLIFFHANGER

## Jacqueline Wilson

*I slipped backwards and suddenly . . . there I was!*
*Suspended. In mid-air. 'Help!'*

From climbing and abseiling to canoeing and a Crazy
Bucket Race, the adventure holiday promises to be full
of action. There's just one problem as far as Tim is
concerned: he is *hopeless* at sports of any kind.

Can Tim survive the horrors of a week absolutely
*packed* with activity? Can his team – the Tigers – be the
overall champions? There are some surprises in store
for everyone!

**From the award-winning author of *The Story of***
***Tracy Beaker*, *The Suitcase Kid* and *Double Act*.**

0 440 86338 4

## ALL TIED UP

Jacqueline Wilson

'Run for it, Lisa!' I shouted. We ran, ran for our lives, charging through the streets of Whitby, the two men close at hour heels.

Gangsters, bank robberies, kidnapping . . . That's not what you expect when you're on holiday in a quiet seaside town. But within twenty-four hours of unpacking, Robert and Lisa find themselves caught up in a wild adventure with a couple of bungling crooks on their tail.

One of the fastest and funniest holiday stories ever!

0 440 86372 4